Lucky Henry Walker, Hurricane Refugee

PRAISE FOR *STORYSHARES*

"One of the brightest innovators and game-changers in the education industry."
– Forbes

"Your success in applying research-validated practices to promote literacy serves as a valuable model for other organizations seeking to create evidence-based literacy programs."

- Library of Congress

"We need powerful social and educational innovation, and Storyshares is breaking new ground. The organization addresses critical problems facing our students and teachers. I am excited about the strategies it brings to the collective work of making sure every student has an equal chance in life."
– Teach For America

"Around the world, this is one of the up-and-coming trailblazers changing the landscape of literacy and education."
- International Literacy Association

"It's the perfect idea. There's really nothing like this. I mean wow, this will be a wonderful experience for young people."   - Andrea Davis Pinkney, Executive Director, Scholastic

"Reading for meaning opens opportunities for a lifetime of learning. Providing emerging readers with engaging texts that are designed to offer both challenges and support for each individual will improve their lives for years to come. Storyshares is a wonderful start."
- David Rose, Co-founder of CAST & UDL

Lucky Henry Walker, Hurricane Refugee

John Porter

STORYSHARES

Story Share, Inc.
New York. Boston. Philadelphia

Storyshares
Story Share, Inc.
24 N. Bryn Mawr Avenue #340
Bryn Mawr, PA 19010-3304
www.storyshares.org

Inspiring reading with a new kind of book.

Interest Level: Middle School
Grade Level Equivalent: 2.7

9781973487654

Book design by Storyshares

Printed in the United States of America

Storyshares Presents

1

Hurricane Katrina struck New Orleans on August 29th, 2005. This storm made landfall as a powerful Category Four hurricane. The City of New Orleans avoided a direct hit from the storm. An extra large surge of water followed this very strong hurricane.

The force of the water surge damaged the levees. Water flowed through the breaks in these walls. Walls to keep water out also keep water in. The pumps to get the water out failed. Low elevation areas were quickly flooded. Some parts of New Orleans were soon under ten feet of water.

People had to flee without their pets. Many would not return. Some would make it back weeks later. Thousands of pets were left behind. This is the story of one family pet's journey.

2

You can call me Lucky. I am a dog living in the city of New Orleans. New Orleans is in the state of Louisiana.

New Orleans is located on the banks of a river. It is a river city. The river is called the Mississippi. The Mississippi River is big, wide and muddy. The Mississippi River flows into the Gulf of Mexico at New Orleans.

We live in the Ninth Ward area of New Orleans. The Ninth Ward has been around for a long time. The houses are older. Ours has a fence around the back yard.

We often cook on the backyard grill. I watch carefully for food to fall off the grill. When food falls, I grab it and run.

The kids and I play fetch with my ball. Playing fetch is fun. Going for a walk is fun. I am on a leash outside the yard. I got a new squeaky toy for my birthday. I am now two dog years old or fourteen human years old. Life is good in New Orleans.

3

A big, scary storm happens. The storm is so strong. There is lots of rain. There is lots of lightning. There is lots of wind. Trees are knocked to the ground. House roofs are torn off. Fences are blown down.

The wind blows open a door to the backyard. Before anyone notices, I go outside. The wind has blown down the fence around the yard. This is my chance to look around.

Should I leave the yard? I am supposed to be on leash. A little look around would be fun. I make a decision. I walk over the fence and down the street.

It is a big mess in our neighborhood. There are big trees lying on the ground. There are branches on roofs. Cars are overturned. The damage goes as far as I can see. There is danger all around.

Hurricane Katrina has made a great big mess. It appears the worst is over. I am several blocks from home. Time to head back to my family.

Before I can get home, the levees break. Water comes rushing into the city. The levee walls can't hold the water back. There is nothing to stop the flooding. The water gets in everywhere. Homes fill up with water and mud. Cars fill up with water. It is really awful.

I finally get back to my block. I can only see the top of my house. The rest of my house is underwater. My family is gone. I don't know where they went. I hope they are safe.

My little walk is not turning out well. Now what should I do? Do I stay around until my family returns, or take off?

I decide to stick around. It is scary to be alone. I do not like being alone. I like my family to be around.

I need to be a brave dog. I must find a way to survive. I need to wait for my family. I need to find food. I haven't eaten for a very long time.

4

I dig in garbage piles to find food. I drink dirty water. Yuck. Bugs bite me all over. My hair and skin are really dirty. I begin to really stink. I am getting really skinny. I see a funny looking scarecrow. I am getting sores on my body. I see some dead dogs and cats. This is not fun. Finding a dry place to sleep is hard. I do not like being alone. How long will I survive?

One day, I see a small pack of dogs. They are a group of refugees like me. The pack leader is nice to me. She is an older female Blue Tick Hound. Being in a pack is better. I am not so lonely.

One day, I get separated from the pack. I do not notice where they are headed. I go up on a hill. I finally see the pack. They are far away by the deep water. Do I stay here or leave?

I see them being picked up by a man. They are being put into a boat. I decide to go with them.

I run down the hill. I swim the deep places. I am too tired to both run and bark. So, I just run as fast as possible. Can I catch them?

I must rest soon. I can't run any longer. But the boat is leaving. I have to stop for a minute. What do I do? I take a deep breath. I bark as loud as possible. I take a breath and bark again.

The man in the front of the boat raises his head. He turns and looks right at me. Then he motions to the other man in the boat. The boat slowly turns and heads my way.

The man in the front of the boat gets out. He wades over to me. He reaches down and picks me up. Being lifted hurts my sores.

Still, being held is the best feeling ever.

5

The men take us to the edge of the flooding. We are then loaded into a big truck. After a long drive, we arrive at our next place.

We are in a big place full of rescued pets. Each of us is given a number. Our rescue location is written on our number tag. My number is five one three three (5133). I was rescued in the lower Ninth Ward of New Orleans, Louisiana.

Each of us is put in a kennel with another dog. We are given clean water. We each have a bowl of clean food. There are dry blankets. I quickly eat and drink. I curl up and fall asleep. I am a very lucky dog.

It is very noisy in the big building. There are hundreds of dogs and cats. We spend most of the day in our kennels. We go outside for a little while three times a day.

Number twenty eight (28) is sharing a kennel with me. Number 28 is a female black Labrador. She is very gentle. We are not real noisy. We do bark sometimes.

There is not much to do. We get pretty bored. What is going to happen next? Where is my family? How will they find me?

One morning, I am put in a crate. A cat is then put in the crate. The crate is lifted with me and the cat inside. We are carried outside.

6

There is a lot of noise outside. We are set down on the ground in our crate. Before long, we are lifted up and placed on a conveyor. This slow-moving, wide belt carries us up to a door. Sixty-eight dogs and thirty-five cats are placed inside the airplane.

I am a little scared. I am also nervous. Are we going far away? I could be really far from home. I have lost my collar. I have lost my tags. No one knows my name or where I live. This is not as scary as being by myself. I do get along with cats.

The plane is really noisy. We get bumped around inside our crates. Where is our plane headed? The plane's tires squeal as the airplane lands. The engines are really loud. The airplane's brakes screech as we stop.

The large cargo door is opened. The unloading equipment is pushed up to the plane. Finally, all the crates are handed down onto the runway. One by one, each of our crates is moved.

We and our crates are placed inside a large building. We have survived this part of our adventure. Where are we? What will happen now? Will we ever get back home?

The Humane Society of Pagosa Springs and the La Plata County Humane Society sponsor our program. They agreed to foster sixty-eight dogs. This a lot of temporary homes. The thirty-five cats are an unexpected bonus. A lot of great humane society volunteers show up to help.

7

All dogs receive a collar. The cats are all taken to a shelter. Dogs are taken for a short walk on leash. Then the lady in charge takes charge.

She says loudly, "Attention, please. Choose a pet you would like to foster. Please get in line to have it bathed. After the pet is clean, have its picture taken."

The lady adds, "After pictures, please get in line for a vet." The boss lady then says, "Each pet will get a full physical. If the pet is healthy, they can go home today. You will get more information after the exam. If you have questions, please ask."

Then she adds in a softer tone, "Your help makes this program possible. Thank you very much."

Many foster families quickly claim the dog of their choice. They get in line for the vet exam. The rest of the families start searching for a dog.

I am so excited to see people. I jump around and bark hello to everyone. I try to lick every person in the building. Who will choose me?

Soon, there are only a few dogs not chosen. Finally, there is only one dog left: me. Did I get too excited?

One last couple arrives and they talk with the lady in charge.

She points at me. I get excited and start to jump up and down. The new lady walks over to me. She quietly says, "settle."

I settle down right away. We go for a short walk with me on leash. Next, we join the line to get me cleaned up. I need a good bath. I get a really good bath. The man bathing me is gentle. I have thousands of insect bites. I have many sores. My hair has fallen out in places. There is a really sore spot on my nose.

I may be skinny and ugly, but I am clean. Many homeless days on the street are bad for a dog's looks.

After the bath, we get in line to see the vet. The vet pokes and feels me all over. A sample of my blood is taken. The vet says to the nice lady, "He will have to have more tests. He will be in the clinic for a few days. We will let you know how he does."

My picture is taken. My number is 5133. The Ninth Ward in New Orleans was my rescue location. My picture and rescue location are put on the internet. There are lost pet sites on the internet. These lost pet sites are so my family can find me. Will my family find me?

The next several days are spent at the vet clinic. There are many tests. I am poked a lot. The tests show I have heartworm disease. I need special medicine. We need to break up the worms. I need to take it easy.

I do have a nice, warm kennel. I have good water and food. I am alone most of the time. The other dogs bark a lot. I do not feel good. I get a lot of sleep in my safe place.

I wake up when my crate is lifted. I am carried away from the clinic. The nice lady from the airport has claimed me. The last dog picked has a foster home.

What do I need to do now? How should I act?

8

The nice woman takes me to her home. She has an old female mutt named Spot. There is also a young female Manchester Terrier named Cricket. Spot is nice to me. Spot shows me where to do things. At first, Cricket is not very nice.

The lady is super nice. She cooks me special food. She puts medicine on my sores. She treats the ringworm on my nose. She cooks seaweed for my bites. She gives me my own blanket. She leaves a light on for me at night. She puts a bone in my safe place, just for me.

The man is nice. He decides to call me Henry. I try to play with Cricket's toys. Cricket gets mad and growls at me. The nice lady gets me my own toy. It looks like a duck. It sounds like a duck. You bite the right place and it honks. I had this kind of toy at home. I offer to share my toy with Cricket. She will not play with it.

Spot does not play with any toys. Spot likes to wear a red bandana around her neck. Some days, I get to wear a green bandana. Spot says I look like a mountain dog. I like to look like a mountain dog. I like to look just like Spot.

The vet tells us I still have heartworm disease. I must not run around. I am supposed to be quiet.

Staying quiet is hard. Heartworm disease is dangerous to my health. I need more shots. I need more worm medicine. The shots sure hurt. I don't feel good.

The nice lady says, "The medicine will make you feel better." My sores are healing. The worms are breaking up.

My hair is looking a little better. I have gained some weight. I can move around a little while each day. I am feeling better. I am not back to my handsome self yet.

One night, a big storm comes. There is lots of thunder and lightning. It is very scary. Spot does not like storms, either. I follow Spot under the bed. I feel much safer. Spot and I are together a lot. We have become good friends.

I need to find a new home. The nice lady is looking for people to adopt me. She promises to take care of me until I am adopted. We have not heard from my family. Where will I go next?

As I feel better, we have visitors. It is fun to meet new people. It is fun to be the center of attention. One family decides to have me over for a visit. They want to see how I do with their dog. My things are packed up.

Spot says to hurry back if I can. She senses a road trip coming up. I can make it back.

The visit does not go well. The family I visit do not like being jumped on. They do not like their slippers chewed. They do not like my fighting with their Collie. I return before dark. Are my adoption chances gone?

Spot is happy to see me back. There is a family trip planned. I get to go along. My heartworms still need to be treated. I still need to be watched. I still need to take it easy. I can only move slowly for a little while. I can't be left alone all night.

We are going to the lady's parents' home for Thanksgiving.

9

The trip is fun. Cricket likes the spot between the front seats. Sometimes, she even gets to ride in the front seat. Spot and I ride in the back seat. We enjoy the ride. We stop for short walks when Spot whines. There is a lot to sniff at a rest stop.

We stay in hotels when it gets dark. I learn not to bark when someone walks by our room. The hallway is not part of our room. I get to ride in elevators. You push a button to go up a floor. You push a button and go down a floor. Elevators can be a lot of fun.

The nice lady's parents do not have a fenced yard. Spot, Cricket, and I get a lot of attention. We are taken everywhere on a leash. I am allowed longer walks each day.

We get to walk in the woods once a day. It is good to sniff a lot. It is good to chase squirrels again. Soon, it is time to head back to Colorado.

Now I know how to act in a rest area. I know how to behave in a car. I know how to be quiet in a hotel. I am not afraid of elevators. Road trips are sure fun.

10

A lady comes to see me soon after our return. She is interested in adopting me. I decide to not behave today. I can't decide if I like her.

I jump up on her lap a couple of times. I rub against her leg a few times. It is hard to settle today. The lady leaves in a hurry. I am told to practice behaving. The man thinks I am deciding who adopts me. He thinks I act badly with some people. He is pretty smart.

We are getting ready for adoption. There is going to be an adoption event for Katrina refugees. Our families have not contacted some of us. My bandana is washed. My coat is brushed. My crate and other stuff are loaded up. Spot and Cricket stay home.

We meet other Katrina refugees that need adopting. We are at a mall in downtown Durango, Colorado. Our crates are placed around the center of the mall. My space is right next to Number 28. We are together again.

Before long, a lot of people come to meet us. A family spends time petting and looking at me. They have three little kids. The kids are pretty gentle. This family goes to see other dogs. A young couple talks with my current nice lady.

The young couple take me outside for a walk. I behave myself. I sit when asked. I lie down when asked. I roll on my back so they can scratch my tummy. These folks have a yard and a cat.

This couple chooses to adopt me. The paperwork is filled out. We get our picture taken. I look almost handsome.

I am so happy. I was the last dog chosen at the airport. I am the first dog chosen today. The second dog adopted today is number 28. She looks pleased with her new lady. She looks pretty good in her picture.

11

I look out the back window of my new car. The nice lady is waving goodbye. The nice man is crying. He is happy for me. He has the remains of my duck. They were very good to me. Spot was really great. Cricket was a little nicer as time passed.

My new family gets my attention as they talk. The lady says, "We need to stop on our way home. He needs a new bowl and a new blanket."

The man says, "He needs a new toy."

My name is now Walker. I am named after a musician. So is Buffett, our cat.

I have been busy since the adoption. I need to be neutered. This is not fun, but it is done. My family decided I needed more schooling. I am now a graduate of Alpine Canine Academy.

My family and I go for long walks. We go to the dog park, where I can really run. Buffett and I play chase around home. We play a lot. We like being together. I hear a new cat may be joining us. That is just fine. I get along well with cats.

I did need more heartworm treatments. My third set of treatments. The vet said I am finally done with the worms. Yeah!

My picture was in the local paper. It is a picture of me sitting on Santa's lap. I really like my new family. I have a great life. I am now Walker the mountain dog.

The La Plata County Humane Society is great. They take my picture with Santa Claus. I like the treat that follows the picture. We go to the pet bakery all year round. We get a supply of fresh baked treats for the week.

I like being a mountain dog. Playing fetch in the snow is great fun. I have a very warm fur coat. I am well suited for the mountains. I have a great mountain family.

I am Lucky Henry Walker.

Lucky Henry Walker

.

About The Author

This is the true story of a Hurricane Katrina rescue dog, as told by John Porter. It has been eight years since Walker was rescued. The Ninth Ward of New Orleans is still recovering from Hurricane Katrina. The levees have been repaired. Many of the homes have not. Many of the residents have not returned.

Extensive efforts were made to reach the families of rescued pets. Written notices were posted in areas where pets were picked up. Directions to the lost pet websites were widely published. Pictures and information on each rescued pet were posted on these websites.

The 103 pets sent to Southwest Colorado soon became 114. One of the dogs was pregnant. She gave birth to 11 puppies two days after arriving in Colorado. Ten of the pets were reunited with their family. Seventeen of the animals died. The remaining 87 were placed in loving homes throughout Southwest Colorado.

The La Plata County Humane Society and The Humane Society of Pagosa Springs made this program possible. Their dedicated staffs and volunteers deserve recognition for their efforts.

Thank you to all involved,

Lucky Henry Walker

About The Publisher

Story Shares is a nonprofit focused on supporting the millions of teens and adults who struggle with reading by creating a new shelf in the library specifically for them. The ever-growing collection features content that is compelling and culturally relevant for teens and adults, yet still readable at a range of lower reading levels.

Story Shares generates content by engaging deeply with writers, bringing together a community to create this new kind of book. With more intriguing and approachable stories to choose from, the teens and adults who have fallen behind are improving their skills and beginning to discover the joy of reading. For more information, visit storyshares.org.

Easy to Read. Hard to Put Down.

Lucky Henry Walker

www.ingramcontent.com/pod-product-compliance
Lightning Source LLC
Chambersburg PA
CBHW071229170626
46809CB00005BA/1983